## A NOTE TO PARENTS

When your children are ready to "step into reading," giving them the right books is as crucial as giving them the right food to eat. **Step into Reading Books** and STAR WARS® **JEDI READERS** present exciting stories and information reinforced with lively, colorful illustrations that make learning to read fun, satisfying, and worthwhile. They are priced so that acquiring an entire library of them is affordable. And they are beginning readers with a difference—they're written on five levels.

**Early Step into Reading Books** are designed for brand-new readers, with large type and only one or two lines of very simple text per page. **Step 1 Books** feature the same easy-to-read type as the Early Step into Reading Books, but with more words per page. **Step 2 Books** are both longer and slightly more difficult, while **Step 3 Books** introduce readers to paragraphs and fully developed plot lines. **Step 4 Books** offer exciting fiction and nonfiction for the increasingly independent reader.

The grade levels assigned to the five steps—preschool through kindergarten for the Early Books, preschool through grade 1 for Step 1, grades 1 through 3 for Step 2, grades 2 through 3 for Step 3, and grades 2 through 4 for Step 4—are intended only as guides. Some children move through all five steps very rapidly; others climb the steps over a period of several years. Either way, these books will help your child "step into reading" in style!

*For my Tali and Gabe—*
*"more than there are stars in the sky"*

*For Robert Shlachter—*
*my cousin and fellow traveler*

*For Fred Lown—*
*my favorite poet*

*For Adine Storer and Ian Magnusson—*
*my neighbors and Star Wars experts*

*And to Heidi Kilgras—*
*my editor and friend—many thanks*
*—E.A.*

www.randomhouse.com/kids
www.starwars.com

Library of Congress Card Number: 00-106290

ISBN: 0-375-80432-3

Printed in the United States of America   October 2000   10 9 8 7 6 5 4 3 2 1
STEP INTO READING, RANDOM HOUSE, and the Random House colophon are registered trademarks and the Step into Reading colophon is a trademark of Random House, Inc.

# JEDI READERS

# STAR WARS

## Darth Maul's Revenge

### A Step 3 Book

by Eric Arnold

illustrated by Tommy Lee Edwards

Random House
New York

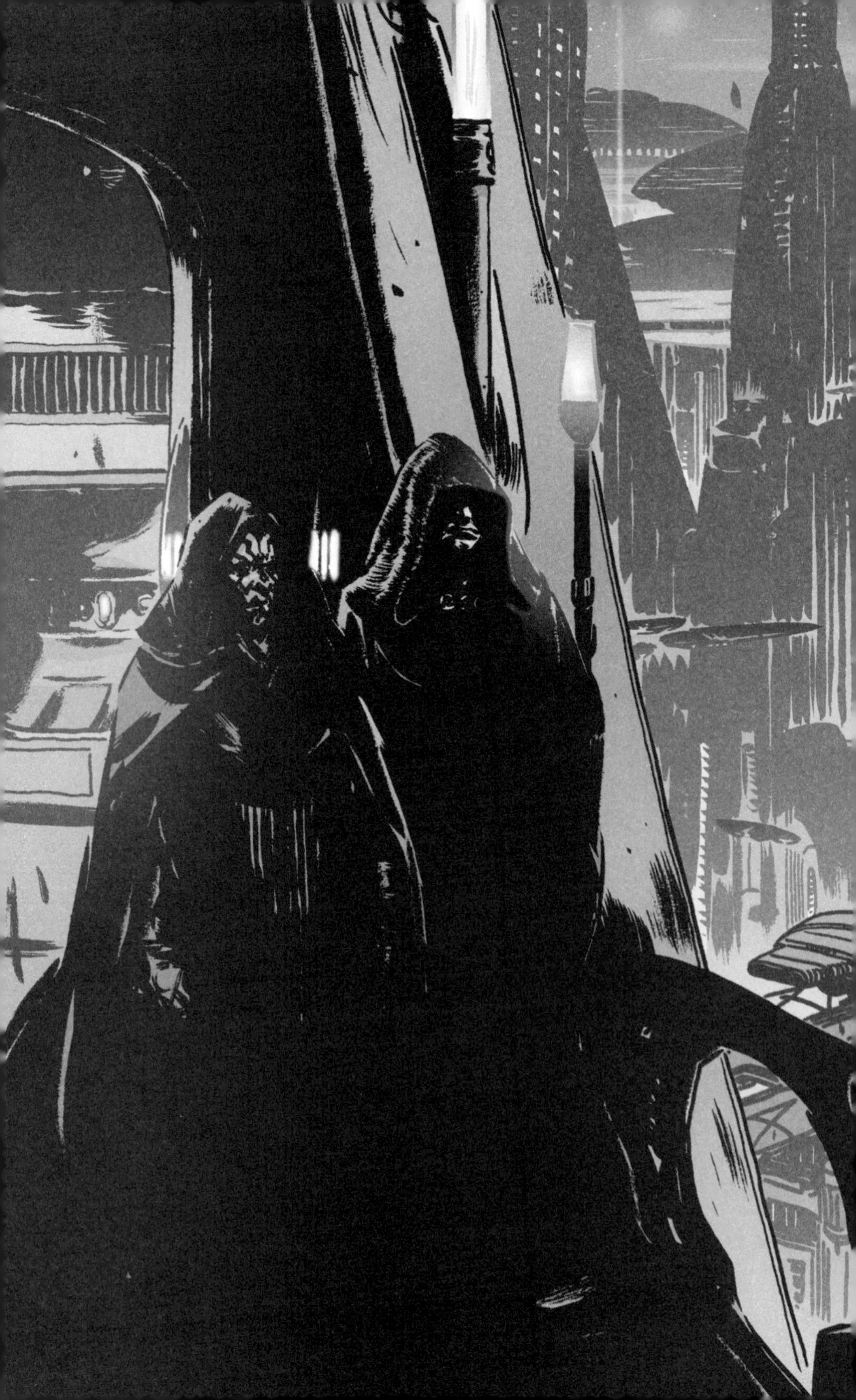

# 1

# The Plan

With his yellow eyes gleaming, Darth Maul glared into the busy night sky over Coruscant—the center of the galaxy.

*Eeeee! Eeeee!*

As hawk-bats flew overhead, Darth Sidious stepped out of the balcony's shadows.

"It has been over one thousand years since the Jedi crushed our kind," Sidious told his apprentice. "But soon it will be *their* turn to be crushed. A new era of Sith rule is about to begin!"

Maul's lips curled with cruel pleasure. "How may I serve you, my master?" he asked.

"Listen closely," Sidious said. "To control the galaxy, we must first control Naboo. And to control Naboo, we must control its Queen. Unfortunately, two Jedi have helped Queen Amidala escape in her Royal Starship. You must find her and take her back to her planet."

Maul checked his wrist comlink for updated information. "If the trace was correct, I will find them quickly, Master. The Queen's starship is headed for Tatooine. It is a bleak planet with few dwellers."

"Move against the Jedi first," Sidious instructed. "Once they are defeated, you will have little trouble taking the Queen back to Naboo."

"At last we will reveal ourselves to the Jedi," Maul said with evil pride. "At last we will have revenge."

Darth Sidious replayed a transmission from Naboo on his holoprojector. Images of the Queen and the two Jedi now protecting her appeared.

At the sight of his enemies, Maul tensed. His Sith training had taught him the art of patience and control. But like an animal ready to spring, he could hardly wait to pounce on his prey.

"You have been well trained, my young apprentice. The Jedi will be no match for you."

As Maul nodded, he slid his hood back, revealing his crown of hooked horns. The Sith apprentice was eager to begin his mission.

# 2
# Sith Infiltrator

*My ship is the fastest in the galaxy, yet it cannot take me to my enemies fast enough,* Maul thought.

His Sith Infiltrator was perfectly designed for sinister missions. And he was the master of its terrifying technology.

*Click!* He put the ship into hyperdrive and it sped through space like a point of light.

With the ship on course, Maul began to check over his equipment.

He displayed images of the two Jedi Knights and Queen Amidala on his holoprojector. He placed this data into his three "dark eye" probe droids.

*My "dark eyes" will find my prey easily,* Maul thought. They could track down almost any life form.

He inspected his electrobinoculars.
They would be perfect for long-distance
scanning—day or night.

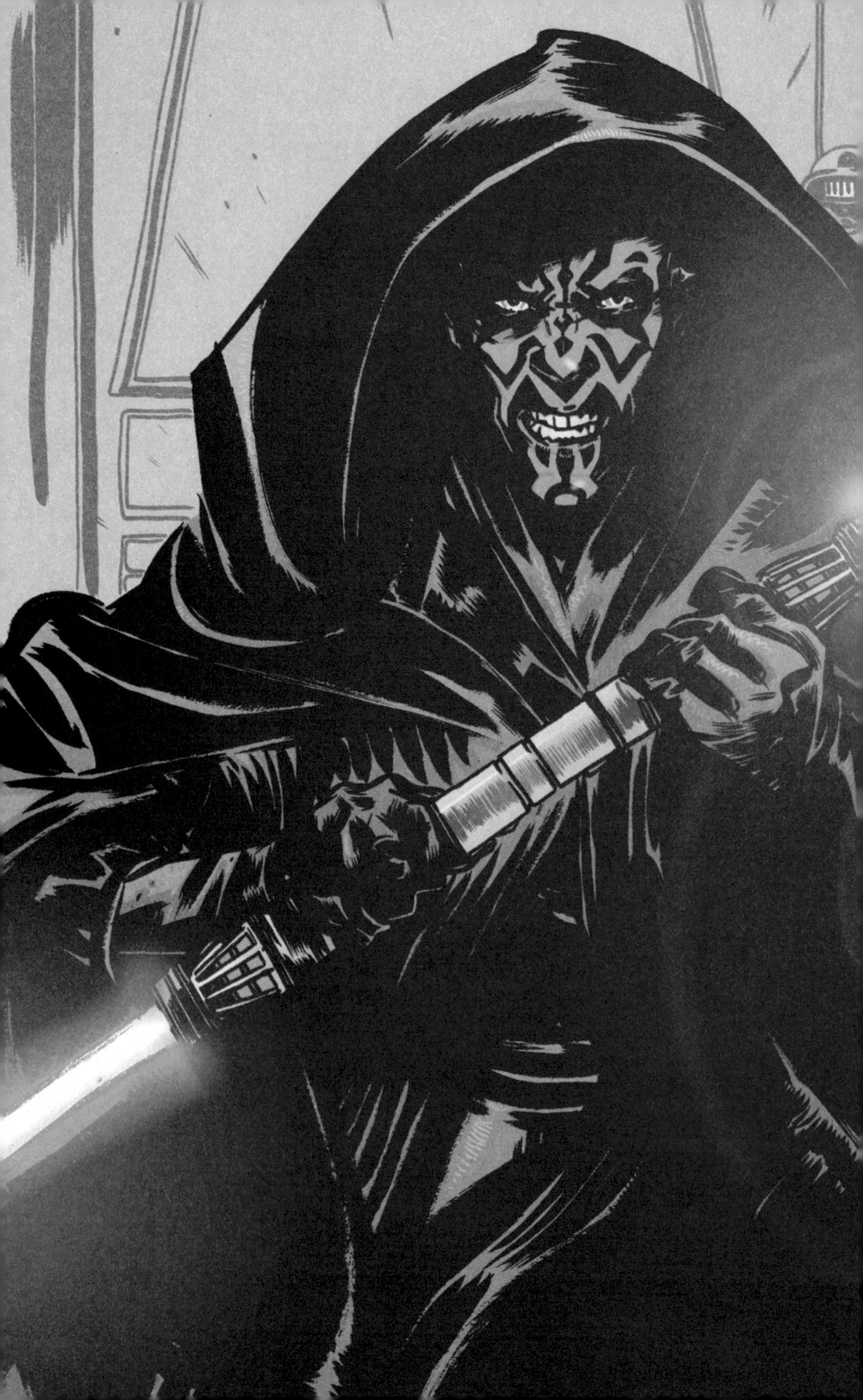

Maul's most prized piece of equipment was his lightsaber. As part of his Sith training, Maul had built his lightsaber by hand. It had two separate blades that could be activated at the same time, making it *twice* as deadly.

Maul released the twin blades, double-checking the weapon. With a quick flick of his wrist, Maul shut down his weapon. His reflexes were as fast as ever.

*My Master has taught me well,* Maul thought with dark satisfaction. *The Jedi will never be prepared for my powers!*

# 3

## Tatooine

Tatooine's two brutal suns had already set
when the Sith Infiltrator neared the edge
of the Dune Sea—a vast desert that
stretched across much of the planet.

*Whooosh…*

A whirlwind of sand scattered as the
craft touched down. The aft hatchway
opened and Maul stepped out into the
darkness.

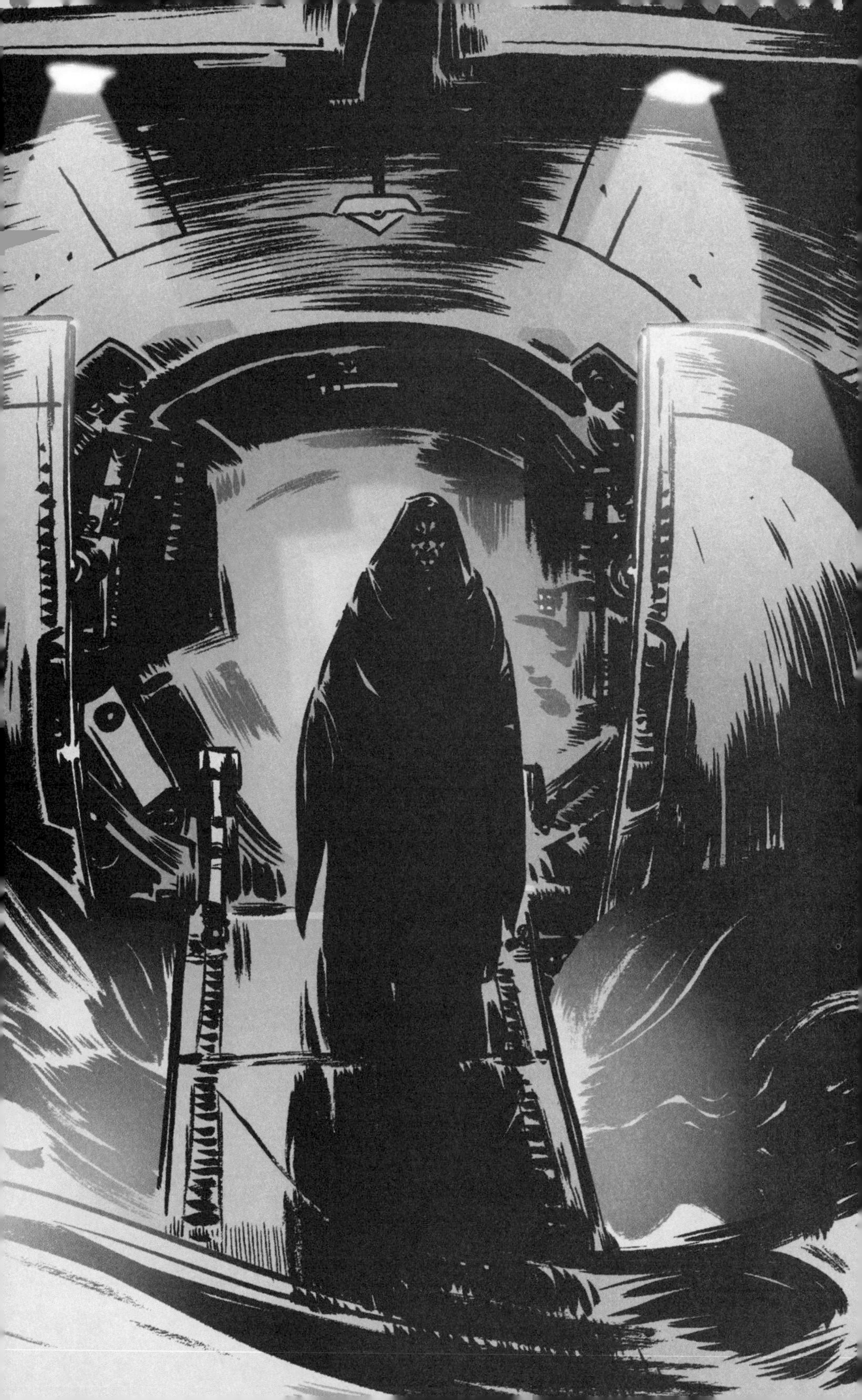

Maul scanned the horizon with his electrobinoculars. A rusted-out sandcrawler sat in the far-off distance. The vehicle was home to Jawas, no threat to the Sith.

Using his wrist comlink, Maul programmed his probe droids to search the three settlements in this area.

*Shweee!* The droids sped toward their destinations under cover of darkness.

*Tracking down the Jedi should be simple enough,* Maul thought. *And once I defeat them, the Queen will be back in my master's hands. I will not fail.*

With the probe droids taken care of, Maul returned to his ship for the night.

The next morning, Maul rose with Tatooine's twin blazing suns. With no news from his probe droids, he decided to practice his Sith arts.

Maul began by focusing his mind on his feelings. Closing his eyes, he thought of the Jedi—and how much he hated them.

A Sith's power comes from the Force's dark side, Sidious had taught him. Fear, anger, and hatred were the keys to that power.

Unlike the Sith, the Jedi drew their strength from peace and justice—the Force's light side.

*Weak fools!* thought Maul.

With lightsaber in hand, he struck at an imaginary Jedi—*swish! swoosh! swash!* Maul handled his lightsaber as if it were a part of his body. The blood red beams sliced the air with pinpoint accuracy.

Next, Maul powered up two deadly assassin droids. Darth Sidious had used similar droids to train Maul when he was a boy.

As the droids rushed toward him, Maul did a double backflip—*fwoop! fwoop!* Using his Sith powers, Maul sprang straight up in the air. He landed on a rocky ledge as the droids rushed past.

Maul cut them to pieces with ease, one after the other. It was over in minutes.

After his training program, Maul began to grow impatient. He was eager to test his skills against a *real* foe.

He paced back and forth in front of the Infiltrator. Suddenly, he spotted something strange near the spacecraft.

Fresh tracks in the broiling sand!
They were bantha prints, and they circled
the Infiltrator. *Is someone spying on me?*
he wondered.

Maul decided to check this out. He
didn't want anything to threaten this
mission.

# 4

# The Ambush

Maul followed the tracks in the sand.
They led him beyond the dunes and into a
canyon.

*This could be a trap,* thought Maul.

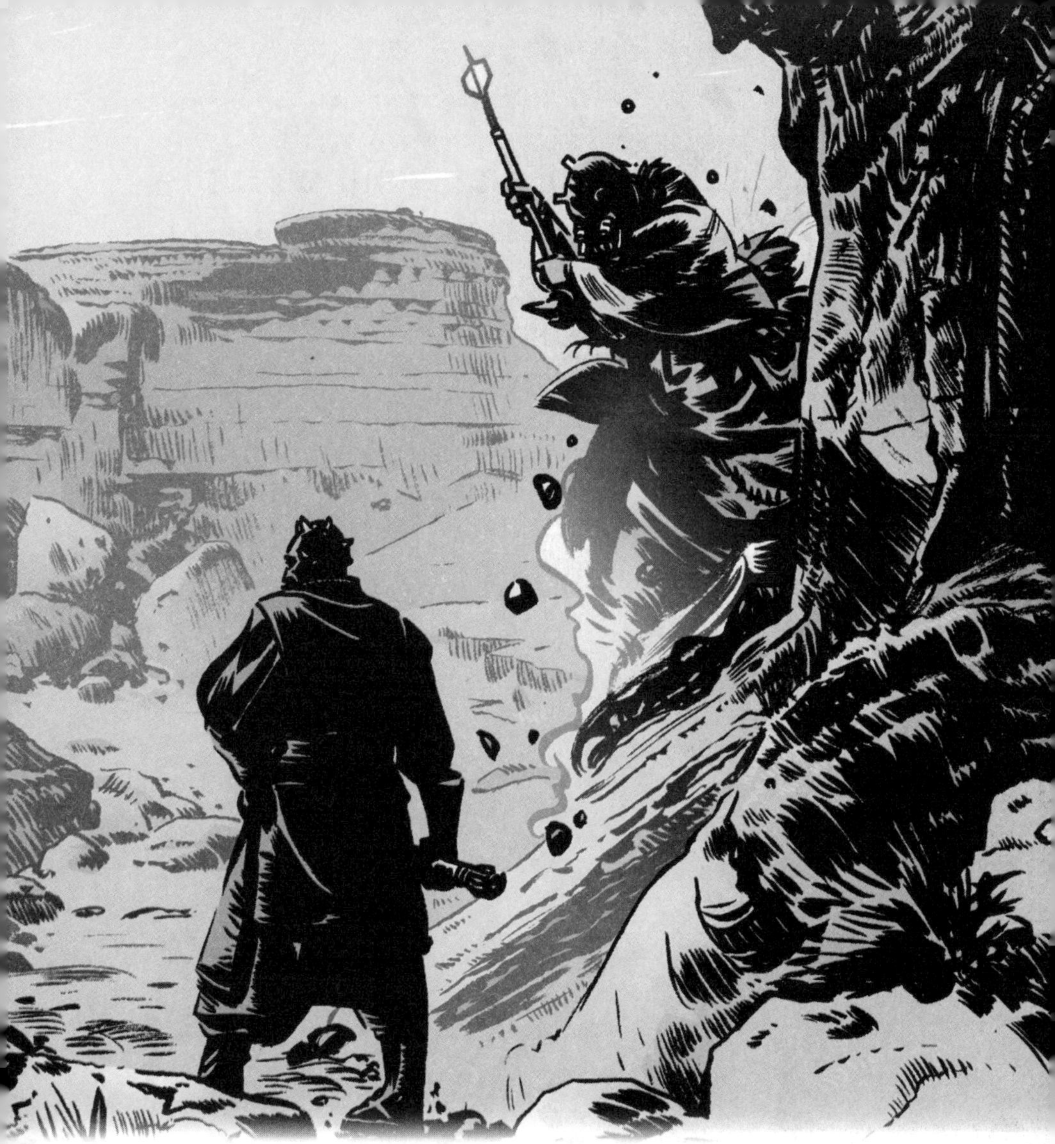

Suddenly, a bantha rounded the canyon wall—but it had no rider. This distracted Maul for just a moment. Out of the shadows burst a Tusken Raider, raising his gaffi stick.

The Raider rushed at Maul with his gaffi stick. In the blink of an eye, Maul activated one end of his lightsaber and sliced the stick in two.

*Defeating this crude being will be no sport at all,* Maul sneered to himself. *It hardly seems worth the effort.*

The gutsy Raider charged again, this time with only half a weapon! But Maul predicted his enemy's every move in advance. He easily blocked the Raider's clumsy attacks again and again.

Just as Maul was about to strike his enemy down, several more Tusken Raiders came out of nowhere! At least thirty of them rushed at Maul from behind rocks and dunes.

He had been tricked!

Maul never ran from a battle. But he could not defeat all *thirty* Raiders.

He should have remembered that Sand People travel in single file to hide their numbers. He had made a foolish error. An error that now endangered his master's mission.

Maul had to get back to his ship. But how? He was surrounded!

The Sand People closed in, swinging their gaffi sticks.

One by one, Maul hacked their sticks in half with his lightsaber. But more Raiders kept coming. They were backing him up against the canyon wall.

*Beeeep! Beeeep!*

Maul's comlink sounded. One of his probe droids had found something!

*These Sand People are tiring me,* Maul realized. *I must save my strength for my mission!*

Trapped against the canyon rock, Maul saw only one way out. Focusing his power, he turned around and ran straight at the wall in front of him.

He ran high up the sheer rockface and did a backward flip.

As a boy, Maul had taken years to master this trick. It had cost him countless bruising falls, but it had been worth it.

With satisfaction, Maul flew through the air and landed *behind* the surprised Raiders! By the time they turned to rush after him, he was already racing back to his spacecraft.

# 5

## Tracked!

Back at the Infiltrator, Maul received a report from one of the probes: the Jedi Master named Qui-Gon Jinn had been spotted walking away from Mos Espa.

*If he's heading out of town on foot, he's probably going to his ship,* thought Maul. *No time to waste!*

Maul rushed to the underside of the craft and removed his speeder bike from the cargo hatch.

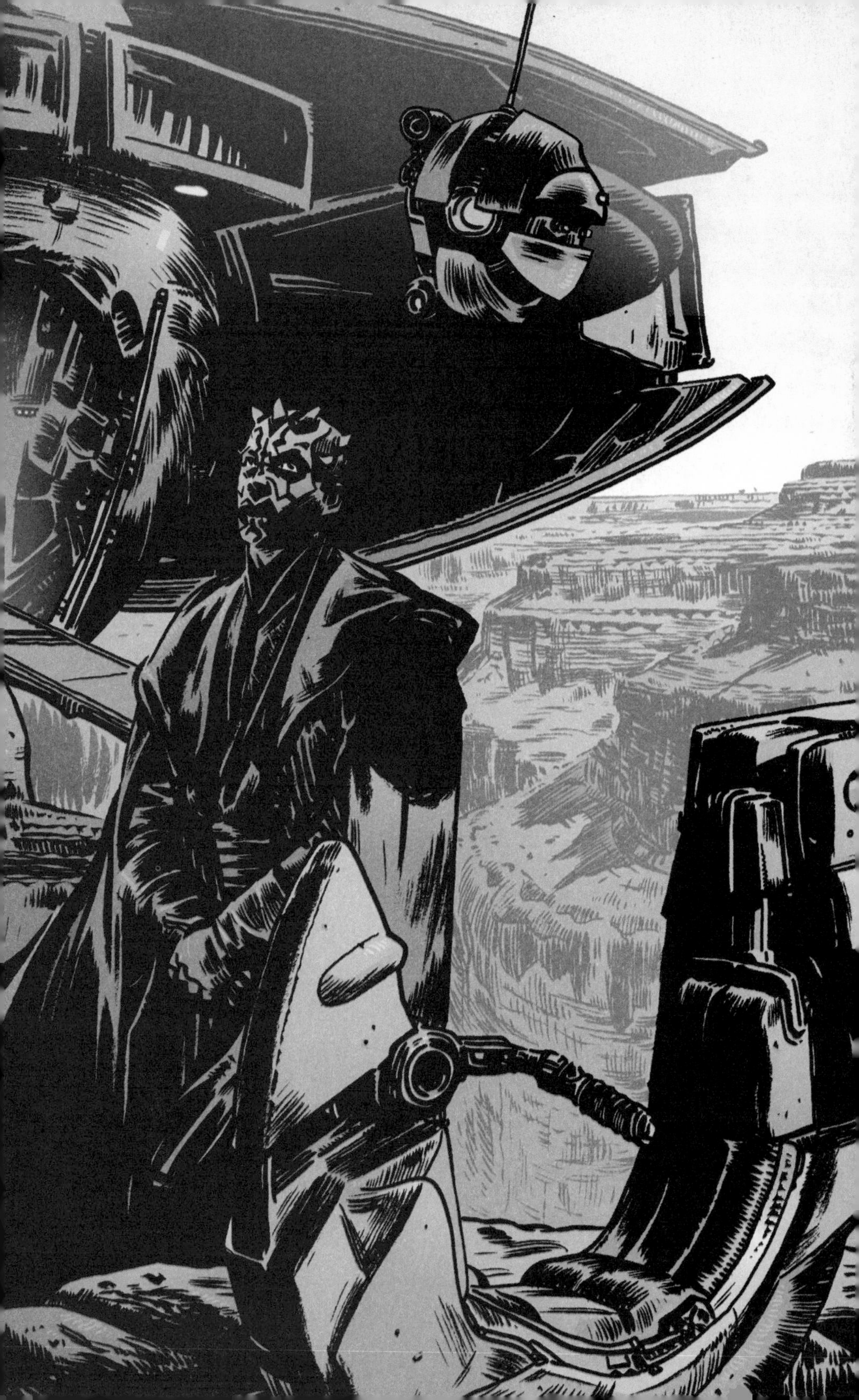

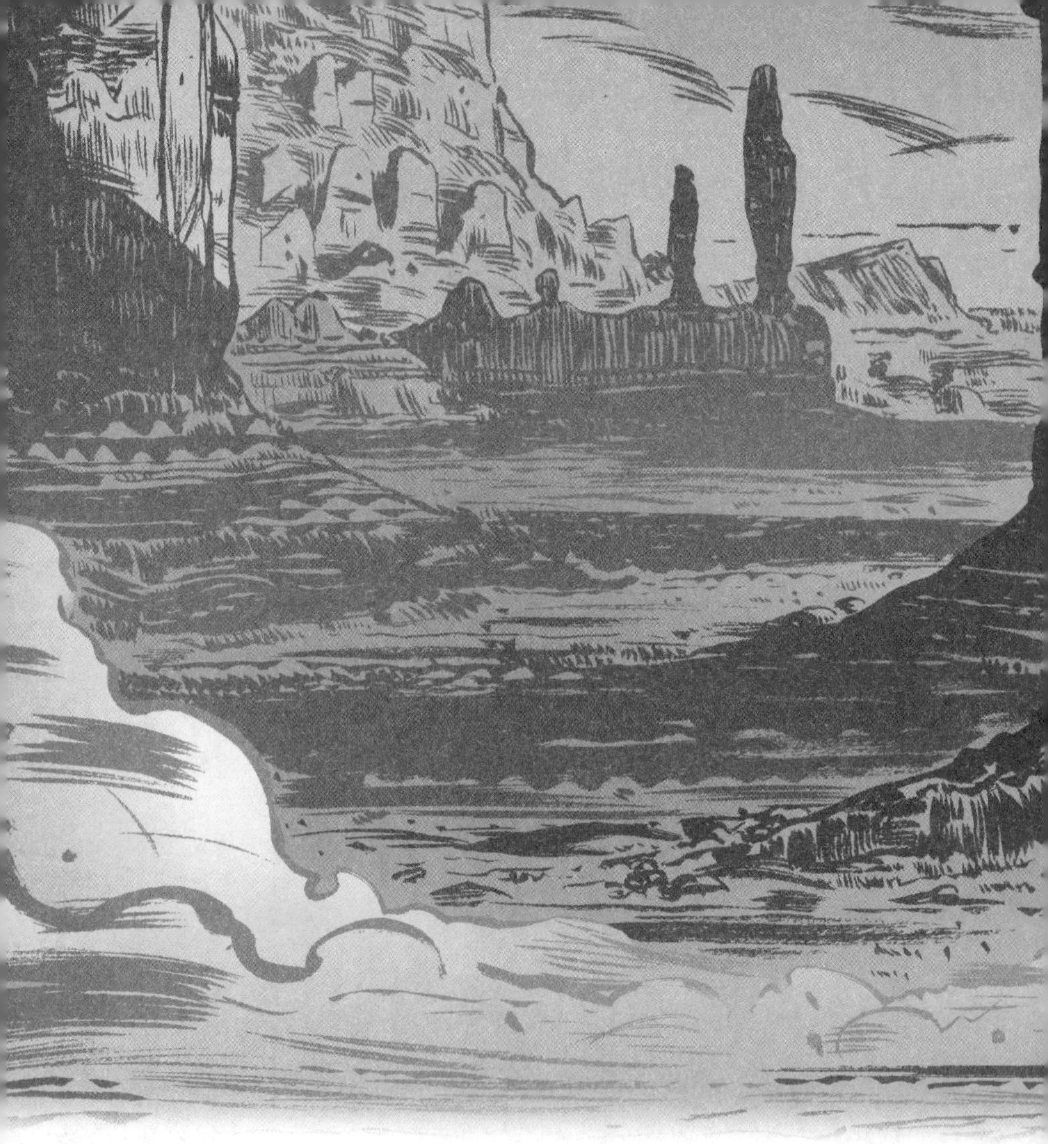

As he raced over the broiling sands of Tatooine, Maul called on his dark powers.

His battle with the Tusken Raiders had been foolish. It had tired him. But Maul vowed it would not slow him down.

He would use his feelings of fury in
the battle. He would pour all of his hate
and anger into his twin blades and cut the
Jedi Master down forever!

# 6
# The Battle

As Maul pushed his speeder to its limits,
he saw two figures running over the
dunes in the distance.

Reaching out with the dark side of the
Force, Maul knew one of these figures
was the Jedi Master Qui-Gon. The other
figure was much smaller—a boy. The
Force was unusually strong in him.

This seemed strange, but Maul could not lose his focus puzzling over a boy. He was closer than ever to his prey!

Maul was almost upon them when the Jedi turned.

"Anakin, drop!" cried the Jedi, spotting the Sith speeder.

The boy fell to the ground just as Maul swept over him!

Maul jumped from his speeder. Before he hit the ground, he swung a powerful blow with his lightsaber.

Qui-Gon barely blocked Maul's blade!

*Be ready for more, Jedi!* Maul growled to himself. He barely noticed the boy picking himself up off the sand.

"Annie, get to the ship!" Qui-Gon yelled. "Tell them to take off! Go!"

Dust kicked up as Maul lunged toward Qui-Gon. The Jedi rolled in the sand to escape Maul's vicious blow. But in an instant, Qui-Gon was back on his feet, swinging his lightsaber.

*Zzzzzzz!* Energy crackled as the blades struck each other.

Maul battled the Jedi with a vengeance. He was surprised at the large man's speed and skill.

*But I am stronger,* thought Maul. *And I can sense surprise in the Jedi. He has never met an opponent like me!*

Maul was pleased by this. Yet he could not find an opening for a final blow. The Jedi was too good.

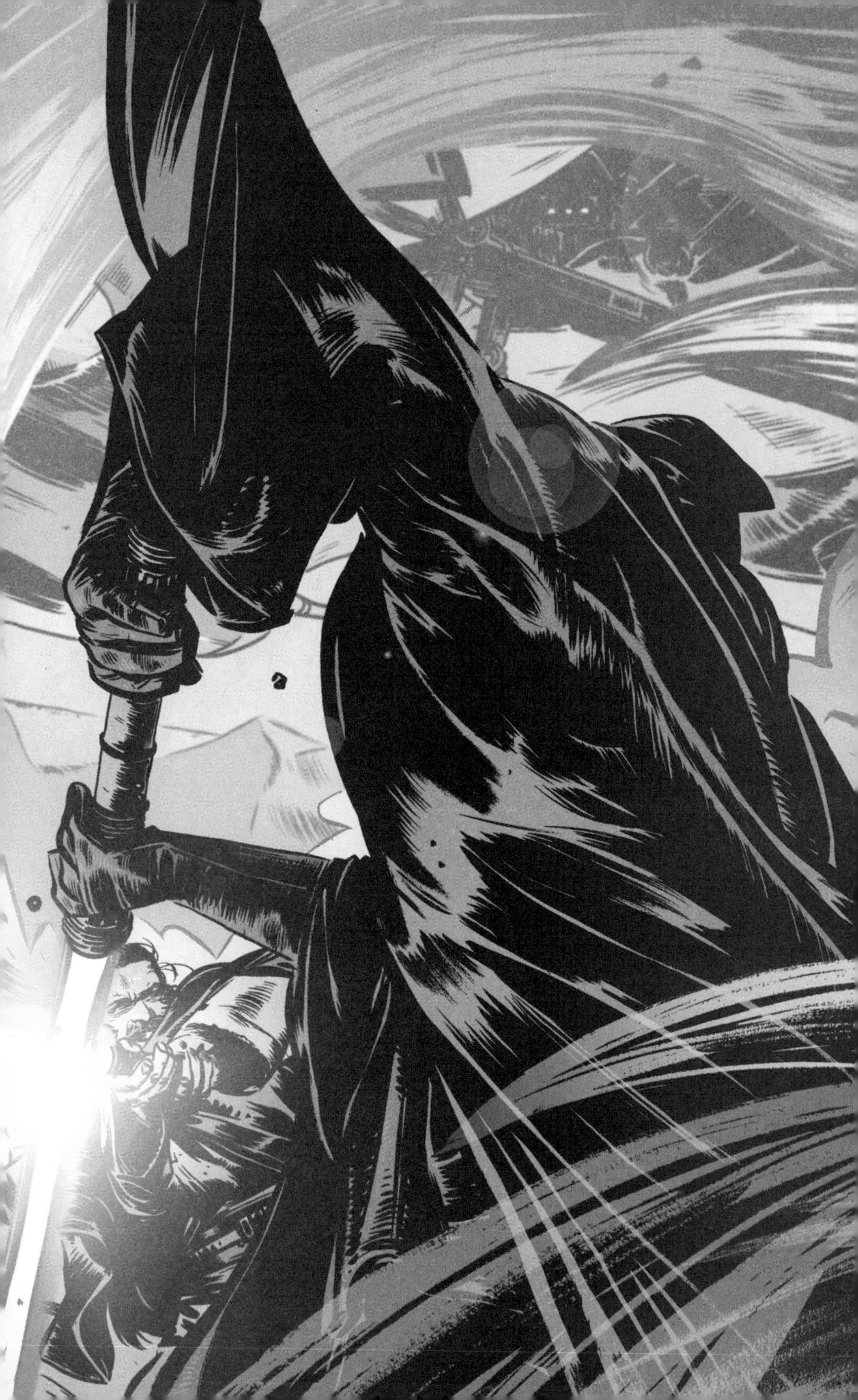

*Whirrrrrrr!* Suddenly, Maul heard the sound of a ship hovering a few feet over their heads. For an instant, he looked up.

In a flash, Qui-Gon jumped to the ramp of the Royal Starship. Before Maul could follow, the ship rocketed away.

*The boy ran for help from the ship,* Maul realized too late.

Stunned, the Sith Lord watched the lights of the engines disappear into the clouds.

The twin suns burned down on Maul's tattooed face, but he did not care. All he felt was the shame of defeat and the need for revenge.

*This battle is not over,* Maul vowed. He and the Jedi would meet again.

*And next time, I will not lose.*